First published in Great Britain in 2010 by Comma Press
www.commapress.co.uk

'Tea at the Midland' by David Constantine © 2010

'Hayward's Heath' by Aminatta Forna © 2010 was first brodcast on
The Verb, BBC Radio 3 on May, 2010.

'Butcher's Perfume' by Sarah Hall © 2010

'If It Keeps on Raining' by Jon McGregor © 2010

'My Daughter the Racist' by Helen Oyeyemi © 2010.

A CIP catalogue record of this book is available from the British
Library.

ISBN   1905583346
ISBN-13   978 1905583348

The publisher gratefully acknowledges the assistance of
Literature Northwest across all its short story projects.

Set in Bembo 11/13 by David Eckersall
Printed and bound in England by SRP Ltd, Exeter

THE BBC NATIONAL SHORT STORY AWARD

2010

Contents

Preface

Judges in any writing competition are doomed to ask themselves one question, and obliged to get it over with as quickly as they can. What makes a good story? In some ways it is a silly question, because a story should describe itself and make its own way in the world. Yet it is inescapable, partly because the question can never be settled. It nags away at you, comes back again and again. And faced with a thick pile of entries for this year's BBC National Short Story Competition we found ourselves feeling the old familiar itch once again. What is it that the best short stories provide?

The readers produced by the BBC and Booktrust had whittled down the entries to a few dozen for us, but there was still such a rich and puzzling mix that all of us – the writers Shena Mackay, Kamila Shamsie and Owen Sheers, Di Speirs of the BBC and myself – found ourselves using the stories to remind ourselves of the difference between writers who understand – *feel* – what the short form can produce, and those who are trying to compress a story into a frame without perhaps having the natural understanding of how a piece of short fiction – the upper limit in the competition is 8000 words – can do something that is particular to the form.

As with all judging panels, we each found ourselves turning over our cards with care, and perhaps sometimes in a teasing or deliberately-misleading way, to try to find out what the others thought. Let's confess that it is fun. We discovered, and this came as no surprise to me, that one of the reasons was that we couldn't be absolutely sure what we felt about many of the stories. There were weak ones, and they fell by the wayside with no tears shed. But the others – a substantial number – were difficult to sort out. We began to talk about what we were trying to find, perhaps what we'd *hoped* to discover in our piles when we started to work our way through the heap. And we found some natural instincts that we all shared.

A short story needs to waste no time. It can't meander, unless the wandering is perfectly controlled and has a hidden purpose. The images, the people, the *mise en scène*, need to spring from the page with clarity and style. And the story must never flag. All of us have favourite short stories from the past by the masters of the form – whether it's F. Scott Fitzgerald or Katherine Mansfield, Saki or Kipling, Poe or Maugham – and we know, as readers, what makes one work. As judges we found in our discussion that although our tastes and stylistic passions are probably quite different, we knew a good one when we saw one.

First of all, we wanted some that didn't drift; that seemed to want to get somewhere. In these stories – from the beginning of Jon McGregor's 'If It Keeps On Raining', for example – you know that you are going to make a discovery. Preferably, a surprising one. That is surely one of the characteristics of most great short stories. I would not be so dogmatic as to insist that revelation is the most important ingredient of short fiction… but surely it is one of the most satisfying feelings to be taken on a journey that lasts only fifteen or twenty pages but nonetheless delivers a narrative that is complete, with a sharpness at the beginning and a feeling of completeness at the end. The short story can expose a writer, cruelly. It takes skill to be able to complete the job, and like a miniaturist on canvas who has to work to distil a world into a few square inches the writer who can suggest a great span in a story that has to be kept in check is a true servant of the craft.

Aminatta Forna's story, 'Haywards Heath', is an example of how a story need lose nothing by being concise. Attila leaps from the pages fully-formed, and there is feeling and menace that ebbs and flows from start to finish. In Sarah Hall's 'Butcher's Perfume', by a writer whose novels have taken her readers on some extraordinarily adventurous journeys, the picture of empty violence and a broken humanity gains power from the compressed scale of the narrative.

These five stories spread widely in their approaches to narrative. 'Tea at the Midland', such an admirably-managed story, has an air of calm in its magical imaginings; Helen Oyeyemi takes quite a different approach in 'My Daughter the Racist', with the shock that so many great writers in this genre create when they turn the world upside down for their own purposes.

As judges, we were inevitably struck by recurring themes that are intriguing and disturbing contemporary writers. Race, splintered families, the loss of innocence in childhood, the plight of the outsider – they are the themes that are most often stirring the imagination of those who put pen to paper in the service of fiction. These five pieces are not the only stories that impressed us, and we're conscious that the obligation to rank pieces of fiction is always an unsatisfactory one. But we know, too, that it is worth subjecting stories to the critical eye, and that judgment matters. There is good and there is bad, and these are good.

This competition has the added dimension of broadcast for the top five stories, and we all know how this form lends itself so often to the enjoyment of the ear. Most of us, I think, recognize that a good story is, in part, one that you can hear in your head.

All of us who had the privilege of reading this year's entries hope that what you hear and what you read gives you great pleasure.

James Naughtie

Tea at the Midland

David Constantine

THE WIND BLEW steadily hard with frequent surges of greater ferocity that shook the vast plate glass behind which a woman and a man were having tea. The waters of the bay, quite shallow, came in slant at great speed from the south-west. They were breaking white on a turbid ground far out, tide and wind driving them, line after line, nothing opposing or impeding them so they came on and on until they were expended. The afternoon winter sky was torn and holed by the wind and a troubled golden light flung down at all angles, abiding nowhere, flashing out and vanishing. And under that ceaselessly riven sky, riding the furrows and ridges of the sea, were a score or more of surfers towed on boards by kites. You might have said they were showing off but in truth it was a self-delighting among others doing likewise. The woman behind plate glass could not have been in their thoughts, they were not performing to impress and entertain her. Far out, they rode on the waves or sheer or at an angle through them and always only to try what they could do. In the din of waves and wind under that ripped-open sky they were enjoying themselves, they felt the life in them to be entirely theirs, to deploy how they liked best. To the woman watching they looked like grace itself, the heart and soul of which is freedom. It pleased her particularly that they were attached by invisible strings to colourful curves of rapidly moving air. How clean and clever that was! You throw up something like a handkerchief, you tether it and by its headlong wish to fly away, you are towed along. And not in the straight line of *its* choosing, no: you tack and swerve as you please and swing out wide around at least a hemisphere of centrifugence. Beautiful, she thought. Such versatile autonomy among the strict determinants and all that co-ordination of mind and body, fitness, practice, confidence, skill and execution, all for fun!

The man had scarcely noticed the surf-riders. He was aware of the crazed light and the shocks of wind chiefly as irritations. All he saw was the woman, and that he had no presence in her thoughts. So he said again, A paedophile is a paedophile. That's all there is to it.

She suffered a jolt, hearing him. And that itself, her being startled, annoyed him more. She had been so intact and absent. Her eyes seemed to have to adjust to his different world. – That still, she said. I'm sorry. But can't you let it be? – He couldn't, he was thwarted and angered, knowing that he had not been able to force an adjustment in her thinking. – I thought you'd like the place, she said. I read up about it. I even thought we might come here one night, if you could manage it, and we'd have a room with a big curved window and in the morning look out over the bay. – He heard this as recrimination. She had left the particular argument and moved aside to his more general capacity for disappointing her. He however clung to the argument, but she knew, even if he didn't know or wouldn't admit it, that all he wanted was something which the antagonisms that swarmed in him could batten on for a while. Feeling very sure of that, she asked, malevolently, as though it were indeed only a question that any two rational people might debate, Would you have liked it if you hadn't known it was by Eric Gill? Or if you hadn't known Eric Gill was a paedophile? – That's not the point, he said. I know both those things so I can't like it. He had sex with his own daughters, for Christ's sake. – She answered, And with his sisters. And with the dog. Don't forget the dog. And quite possibly he thought it was for Christ's sake. Now suppose he'd done all that but also he made peace in the Middle East. Would you want them to start the killing again when they found out about his private life? – That's not the same, he said. Making peace is useful at least. – I agree, she said. And making beauty isn't. 'Odysseus welcomed from the Sea' isn't at all useful, though it is worth quite a lot of money, I believe. – Frankly, he said, I don't even think it's beautiful. Knowing what I know, the thought of him carving naked men and women makes me queasy. – And if there was a dog or a little girl in there, you'd vomit?

She turned away, looking at the waves, the light and the surfers again, but not watching them keenly, for which loss she hated him. He sat in a rage. Whenever she turned away and sat in silence he desired very violently to force her to attend and continue further and further in the thing that was harming them. But they were sitting at a table over afternoon tea in a place that had pretensions to style and decorum. So he was baffled and thwarted, he could do nothing, only knot himself tighter in his anger and hate her more.

Then she said in a soft and level voice, not placatory, not in the least appealing to him, only sad and without taking her eyes off the sea, If I heeded you I couldn't watch the surfers with any pleasure until I knew for certain none was a rapist or a member of the BNP. And perhaps I should even have to learn to hate the sea because just out there, where that beautiful golden light is, those poor cockle-pickers drowned when the tide came in on them faster than they could run. I should have to keep thinking of them phoning China on their mobile phones and telling their loved ones they were about to drown. – You turn everything wrongly, he said. – No, she answered, I'm trying to think the way you seem to want me to think, joining everything up, so that I don't concentrate on one thing without bringing in everything else. When we make love and I cry out for the joy and the pleasure of it I have to bear in mind that some woman somewhere at exactly that time is being abominably tortured and she is screaming in unbearable pain. That's what it would be like if all things were joined up.

  She turned to him. What did you tell your wife this time, by the way? What lie did you tell her so we could have tea together? You should write it on your forehead so that I won't forget should you ever turn and look at me kindly. – I risk so much for you, he said. – And I risk nothing for you? I often think you think I've got nothing to lose. – I'm going, he said. You stay and look at the clouds. I'll pay on my way out. – Go if you like, she said. But please don't pay. This was my treat, remember. – She looked out to sea again. – Odysseus was a horrible man. He didn't deserve the courtesy he received from Nausikaa and her mother and father. I don't forget that when I see him coming out of hiding with the olive branch. I know what he has done already in the twenty years away. And I know the foul things he will do when he gets home. But at that moment, the one that Gill chose for his frieze, he is naked and helpless and the young woman is courteous to him and she knows for certain that her mother and father will welcome him at their hearth. Aren't we allowed to contemplate such moments? – I haven't read it, he said. – Well you could, she said. There's nothing to stop you. I even, I am such a fool, I even thought I would read the passages to you if we had one of those rooms with a view of the sea and of the mountains across the bay that would have snow on them.

She had tears in her eyes. He attended more closely. He felt she might be near to appealing to him, helping him out of it, so that they could get back to somewhere earlier and go a different way, leaving this latest stumbling block aside. There's another thing, she said. – What is it? he asked, softening, letting her see that he would be kind again, if she would let him. – On Scheria, she said, it was their custom to look after shipwrecked sailors and to row them home, however far away. That was their law and they were proud of it. – The tears in her eyes overflowed, her cheeks were wet with them. He waited, unsure, becoming suspicious. – So their best rowers, fifty-two young men, rowed Odysseus back to Ithaca over night and lifted him ashore asleep and laid him gently down and piled all the gifts he had been given by Scheria around him on the sand. Isn't that beautiful? He wakes among their gifts and he is home. But on the way back, do you know, in sight of their own island, out of pique, to punish them for helping Odysseus, whom he hates, Poseidon turns them and their ship to stone. So Alcinous, the king, to placate Poseidon, a swine, a bully, a thug of a god, decrees they will never help shipwrecked sailors home again. Odysseus, who didn't deserve it, was the last.

He stood up. I don't know why you tell me that, he said. – She wiped her tears on the good linen serviette that had come with their tea and scones. – You never cry, he said. I don't think I've ever seen you cry. And here you are crying about this thing and these people in a book. What about me? I never see you crying about me and you. – And you won't, she said. I promise you, you won't.

He left. She turned again to watch the surfers. The sun was near to setting and golden light came through in floods from under the ragged cover of weltering cloud. The wind shook furiously at the glass. And the surfers skied like angels enjoying the feel of the waters of the Earth, they skimmed, at times they lifted off and flew, they landed with a dash of spray. She watched till the light began to fail and one by one the strange black figures paddled ashore with their boards and sails packed small and weighing next to nothing.

She paid. At the frieze a tall man had knelt and, with an arm around her shoulders, was explaining to a little girl what was going on. It's about welcome, he said. Every stranger was sacred to the people of that island. They clothed him and fed him without even asking his name. It's a very good picture to have on a rough coast. The lady admitted she would have liked to marry him but he already had a wife at home. So they rowed him home.

Haywards Heath

Aminatta Forna

THE CAR RADIO issued a blast of sound so sudden and brutish that Attila nearly came to an emergency stop. It took a moment to gather himself. In his chest his heart beat wildly and his scalp had shrunk against his skull, hair follicles tightened in alarm, altogether a sign he was more nervous than he let himself believe, though in every other way he was feeling pretty good about things. The weather, for one: a cool, clear Spring day. The prospect of the drive on clean-surfaced, empty roads. An escape from the city, time to himself.

The youth at the car hire desk must have turned on the radio when he brought the car around. The new generation could not tolerate the sound of silence. This was the second car, there having been little possibility of Attila's bulk being contained by the first. The desk clerk had failed to see what a fool could not have missed. Still, had it been otherwise he wouldn't be driving a Jaguar XJ

from the Prestige range for the same price. Attila
fiddled with the radio until he found something
pleasing. Gradually he felt his scalp withdraw its
grip on his cranium.

At Crawley he left the M23. He thought he
should eat and turned off the main road towards
Haywards Heath. Haywards Heath. It had been a
joke between he and Rosie for a long time. The
overseas students all had a hard time pronouncing
it. Ay-wads 'eat. A sly tease, she would ask each new
acquaintance to repeat the name of her hometown.
After his turn she'd glanced at him over her sherry
glass and he held her gaze until she turned away.
He knew, from the way she stood, the way she
walked, mostly from the way she refused to turn
back in his direction, that she felt the mark of his
gaze on her skin, like a touch on the back of her
neck. Afterwards and perversely, many months into
their affair, she denied she'd noticed him that
evening. He wore a Malcolm X goatee and a suit
to attend lectures. This made her feel sorry for him,
she said. They were in their third year when they
met, together for three more. By the time of their
graduation ceremony he was already six thousand
miles away.

At the London hospital where he worked as
a visiting consultant – visits which had occurred
twice yearly for the last five years, because of his
expertise in displaced populations, in trauma – he
had exhaled all the breath in his lungs at the sound

of her name. Early retirement, his colleague replied in answer to Attila's careful enquiries. The idea for the trip came to him in a moment and had taken over. He had been consumed by the details: renting the car, planning the route, driving on the left hand side of the road.

He thought again about food. At a pub he pulled over and parked. Inside he found a booth and ordered orange glazed duck, which arrived garnished with a rose of tomato peel, which he also consumed. He drew no stares. He opened the atlas out on the table. He reckoned he was less than five miles away. After he had eaten he carried the map to the publican, who jerked his head at the Jaguar and said: 'What no SatNav? Where you headed?'

'Haywards Heath,' pronounced Attila, perfectly.

Next to Attila in the passenger seat the publican pushed the buttons of the device and rubbed the tips of his fingers along the wood of the dashboard. Guided by the patient, electronic voice Attila passed through one village and then another. When he missed a turning the voice redirected him in the same even tone. Attila found himself unaccountably irked by the smoothness of her voice. He took another wrong turn, quite deliberately. She proved unflappable.

Now he knew how his patients felt. He analysed his own behaviour. Prevarication. He drove steadily for ten minutes following the voice's orders.

'You have arrived at your destination.'

What had he imagined? A bungalow. Shelves of books and papers. A quiet, ordered existence writing for professional journals. Some vanity constrained his imagination before it could reach the point of giving her a husband.

Rosie hadn't published in years.

At the desk he asked for her by her maiden name.

'Are you a relative?' asked the woman, unblinkingly.

Attila hesitated. The woman was black herself. A young, African man in a white nurse's uniform moved noiselessly across the hall carpet. 'A friend,' Attila said, finally.

'In the day room.'

The air was over heated, filled with static and the smells of cooked food and talcum powder. Nobody minded him as he moved heavily through the building. In the day room residents slept in the pale sunlight. Others were gathered in a semi circle around a radio. He found her by the window, a newspaper on her lap. She hadn't noticed him. In that moment he was aware of the possibility of turning back, and also of all he had to say. All that had happened, the foreseen and the unforeseen. He wished now he had brought something, flowers or chocolates.

'Hello, Rosie.' When she didn't respond, he moved into the line of her vision.

Now she looked directly at him: 'Hello,' she said and smiled.

'Hello, Rosie,' he repeated. He stood, his hands by his side. He smiled, too and shook his head. 'How are you?'

'I'm very well,' she nodded.

'Your former colleagues helped me find you.' He moved to sit next to her.

'Did they?' She didn't turn to him, and so he examined her offered profile for a few moments. How much beauty there was still. Spontaneously he took her hand. His greatest fear had been that an excess of courtesy would surround their meeting. The last time they saw each other she had not wanted him to leave. He told her it was a condition of his scholarship. They'd argued for weeks, months. What about us? she'd pleaded. But he went back to his country anyway, full of ideas of himself, of the future. Which one of them had been naive?

They sat in silence and the silence felt comfortable already.

'Are you married?'

'I was,' replied Attila. 'She died.'

'Ah, I'm sorry.' She tutted and shook her head. 'That must have been difficult for you.'

He said nothing. The events had unfolded on news programmes around the world, he'd wondered then why she never made contact.

Outside an elderly resident on a bench threw crumbs for a lone blackbird. Next to her a young woman turned away to speak into a mobile phone, her free hand thrust deep into the pocket of her coat. Where to begin?

In the end he said simply: 'I'm sorry. I'm sorry I didn't stay, *that* I didn't stay,' He waited for her response in silence. She must know exactly what he meant. It's what he came here to say, though he had not, until this moment, admitted it to himself.

She patted him on the arm with her free hand and the action brought him comfort. 'It's alright.' They sat once more in silence. When she spoke she said: 'I'm afraid you'll have to tell me your name again, dear.'

He closed his eyes and breathed deeply: 'Attila.'

She smiled, 'I have a friend with the same name. What a coincidence! He's coming to see me any time soon. I'm waiting for him. Maybe you two will meet.'

'Excuse me.' He rose and went in search of the men's room. Inside he leaned his back against the cubicle door until he gained some control of his breathing. The temperature in the place had brought him out in a sweat. He washed his hands and loosened the collar of his shirt. After he left the lavatory he didn't return immediately to the day room, but roamed the ground floor of the building.

Through a porthole in a door he saw the young African helper spooning food into the mouth of an elderly woman. Something about the scene stopped Attila: the hand at her back, which prevented her from slumping, the infinite care in the way the young man wiped her slackened mouth with a napkin. At one point the careworker looked up, straight at Attila. Their eyes met. The young man said nothing but bent once more to his task. Attila turned away.

To Rosie he suggested a walk in the grounds and was relieved when she accepted.

'How long have you lived here?'

She misunderstood and replied: 'Since I was a girl. In Hayward's Heath. What about you?'

'I went to university near here. It was a long time ago.'

But she was already distracted: 'People say you can't have two robins in the same garden, but there's no truth in it. Look!' And then: 'A wren. I do believe there are more of them than there were twenty years ago.'

She held onto his arm, seemingly awash with the wonder of it all. She reached out to touch the drops of rain on the leaves, tilted her head, gazed at the sky and closed her eyes. He waited and watched her. She stretched out her arms. He had a memory of a photograph of her in the exact same pose. Where was it now? She let her arms drop back to her sides. They completed a first tour of the garden. Rosie said: 'Shall we do another turn, Attlia? Another turn?' It was a phrase she had used often in the past: at the funfair, boating on a lake, on a dance floor. She teased him for being too serious.

Attila felt light-headed and – somewhat bizarrely – youthful. It was the effect of Rosie's mood, her enthusiasm for this unremarkable, chrysanthemum bordered square of lawn, also the fact of being the youngest in the place by twenty years, excepting the staff. Fewer silver strands in Rosie's dark hair than in his own. He remembered she had no brothers and sisters.

They passed for the second time the woman on the bench, her daughter still speaking on the telephone. Rosie bent forward, plucked a sweet from the box on the old woman's lap and popped it into her mouth. Rosie gave an impish giggle, the sweet bulged in her cheek. 'She won't miss one. They're my favourite.' She gripped his arm and leaned her head against his shoulder. He inclined his head to hers and smelt the faint brackish odour of her hair, resisted the urge to kiss it. Behind them the old woman sat staring into the middle distance her hands curled limply around the box of sweets. Attila could hear the daughter finish her call.

'Promise you'll come and visit me again, won't you?' Rosie said suddenly, raising her head. 'It's deathly dull in here.'

He gave his promise and meant it. Perhaps if

he kept coming she would eventually remember him, as she almost had today. On this slender hope he hung his heart.

Two months later he returned carrying a box of Newbury Fruits. The sweets had not been especially easy to find and the packaging had changed, as might be expected after forty years. Along the way he had stopped at the same pub, where the publican remembered him or, more accurately, the Jaguar which had been replaced by a Vauxhall for this trip. Rosie wasn't in the day room, nor in the garden though the weather was fine enough to permit it. Attila retraced his steps back towards reception. The woman, a different one to before, angled her head in the direction of a corridor. Attila advanced down it, bearing the box of sweets clamped in his huge hand.

In the dining room he found an afternoon dance underway: a dozen people moved slowly to the sound of the Blue Danube. Mostly residents danced with a member of the staff. Around the room elders dozed and snored, made soporific as flies by music and heat.

There in the centre – Rosie, cradled by the arms of the young, African worker Attila had noticed during his last visit. Her forehead was pressed against his chest, her hand in his, eyes closed. The care worker had his head bent towards her. He had young, smooth skin and, Attila noticed for the first time, a small beard.

For some minutes Attila stood and watched. Then he placed the box of sweets down on a table and reached for a chair. As he did so, the music wound to a halt, people began to shuffle from the floor. He bent to pick up the box of sweets, heard Rosie say his name and looked up. The smile was already on his face.

But she was not looking his way, seemed not to be aware of his presence in the room. Rather she was looking up at the young careworker, who still held her in his arms. 'Shall we do another turn, Attila? Another turn. What do you say?'

And the young man replied: 'Whatever makes you happy, Rosie.'

Rosie nodded. The music began again. Attila replaced the box of Newbury Fruits on the table. He sat down and watched.

Butcher's Perfume

Sarah Hall

LATER, WHEN I knew her better, Manda told me
how she'd beaten two girls at once outside the
Cranemakers Arms in Carlisle. She said all you
had to do was keep hold of one, keep hold of one
and keep hitting her. No matter what the other
was doing to you, you kept that first one pinned,
and you kept hammering her, so the free-handed
bitch could see you were able to take a flailing
and still have her mate at the same time. It'd get
into the lass's head then, Manda said, what it
would be like when the mate got put down, and
you went to batter her next without a silly dog
on your back making you slow. Chances were you
wouldn't have to fight them both. And if you did,
that second one would be so fleart from you
being still upright after her best, undefended go,
she'd forget any moves she knew.

Manda was fiercer than all of us. It had
nothing to do with her size – it never does with

girls, for the willowy tall ones are often gentle as
you like. Manda was small – maybe five foot two.
She wasn't squat either, not pelvic, or thick with
glands and brawn. It was in her eyes. She had eyes
that got set off easily, like a dog chained up all its
life and kicked about, prone to attack for no other
provocation than it catches you looking its way.
All you can do is pray the chain holds at the stake.
And it was in her brain. She didn't have a switch
in there that stopped her from pulling back her
fist, like the rest of us. That's why we were all
afraid of her. That's why her name went before
her – Amanda Slessor – and if you heard it said in
a room you felt ill at ease, you felt things shift out
of the way for its coming into the conversation.
Everyone knew she was hard. It was the first
thing ever they knew about her. It was her
pedigree.

People said she was raised to it, with that
family of hers. There was a lot of arrogance and
expectation mixed up in the Slessors. They were
known for prison sentences, and pig-iron money
that built them a big house above the town's
industrial estate. They had reputations for fertility
at every age, for a seed that always took, and a
womb that always produced – thirteen and virgin
to those traveller grandmothers suckling at fifty.
The town thought it understood their cause –
they'd been forged from the old rage of the
North, it was said. They were not drovers or

farmers, nor the quiet settlers of the Borders. They came from gipsy stock, scrappies, dog- and horse-breeders, fire-mongers.

These were the ones that lit the beacons when other folk hid in cellars and down wells. They smeared offal on their chests and waited at the citadel with their bearded hounds for the Scots. These were the ones who took trophy heads and played football with them in the streets. They had Pictish hearts that allied with an enemy for the sake of avoiding slaughter, but never forgot the original blood of their tribe. And a generation on, at the turning of the Solway tide, there would be a reckoning. The men would take up arms. The women would braid boars' hair into their own. They'd murder their infants birthed to the off-coming sires. Where does history end, we were once asked in school.

'With the Muslims,' some clever-arse shouted.

You may as well ask where true north begins.

The father, Geordie Slessor, went about town like the next in line for the throne, beating the Duke of Edinburgh every year at the local horse driving trials with a trap team of Heltondale Fells reared from his own Entires. Come June you'd see him practising along the roads, green-Barboured, leaning back from the reins. He was gristle right through to the bone. The brothers were fighters too, the three of them, and they all had the same eyes as Manda, got from their gipsy mam: healthy blue, polished up to a high gleam, and set against bad skin. Manda was the sole daughter and she had her own tough clave quality that went beyond family; something not inherited, something made perfectly for hitting off another surface. You'll think me a daft mare for saying that. But sometimes there's strange beauty up here. It's found in deep cut places. It's found in the smoke off the pyres and the pools on the abattoir floor.

Past their notoriety I knew nothing of the Slessors. When I went to the secondary school all I had to go by was common judgment and the air rucking up at the sound of their name. I was late for catching my bus home when I first came across Manda's group. The last bell had cleared the yard, except for a ring of girls by the playground wall, hair short and stiff, skirts high on their thighs. Their heels were scuffling and scraping on the tarmac. They'd got Donna Tweddle alone, tracked her down after a week's tortuous promise of some retribution, for whatever reason she'd offended them: brains, looks, a boy. Manda was holding her by the throat and Donna drooped like rabbit-skin, like carrion. Her jaw was working up and down as she cussed. She knew her way round language I'd only heard outside the bookies or on building sites, things I'd only heard grown men say before. She was loud in what she was doing, but she was bonny in it too.

'You're a lajful little tuss,' she told the girl in her grip. 'Aren't you?'

Her face wasn't pretty and smiling the way lads like girls' faces to be. Manda had her good features, those clear firedog eyes among them, and a heavy chest at fifteen, but that wasn't it. What she was doing suited her, and she was lit up, the way someone plain looks better when they sing, when suddenly it seems they have bright colours under a dull wing.

The girl was strung up against the pebbledash. I don't know if she'd tried to rail against the attack or to reason, but now she was holding still. Then Manda delivered a slap to her face. It was already aflame from her panic-blush, but the clean leather crack of that hand marked it scarlet. There was no real damage done. Manda waited until Donna began to cry, and at that point the viciousness left her. She scratched a place under her chin, letting go of the girl's neck as she did so, as if she'd lost interest in finishing the lass off. As if she couldn't be bothered. The brightness left her. Until that point she'd been full of glister. The girls in the group laughed and sang a last threat or two to Donna. Then their attention turned.

I'd stopped walking. I hadn't hurried away as I should have done, given such a situation. Manda Slessor faced me too. I was in her year at school but she didn't know me. I was a middle-row sitter, a nondescript. I thought she might shove me over or shoulder past. She did push others standing around her after she was done brawling, if they weren't on her side, if the temper was still in her. She saw me looking. I knew I shouldn't be, but I couldn't help it; I couldn't help thinking how bright she'd seemed. Her eyes curtsied quickly up and down, taking me in, a head to toe look in less than a second that said she didn't particularly like what she saw but it was no offence to her. I could feel the air all around, its softness, and in it the two of us were free to move. Her mascara was smudged in the corners from the day's wear. Her eyes were dark petrol blue, oily and volatile, ready to flare up and burn again. But they didn't ignite. She picked her canvas tote up off the ground and walked right past me.

★

I spent time up at the Slessors' house: *Nine Chimneys* it was called. I spent time with the family, after school and on weekends, whenever I could, because I didn't want to stay out in the village I was from with my dad being moody and nobody else my age. How it all came about I couldn't exactly say. The friendship was suddenly there one day, slightly askew in the beginning, like a sapling on the verge, then stronger and straighter. Maybe I was just someone she didn't get into a lock with, and that meant we weren't enemies. Or maybe she saw something she liked that day in the yard. She saw my admiration.

One day she caught me watching her eat a packet of crisps, licking salt off her fingers, and she blew me a kiss across the canteen as if she thought I fancied her. She could be daft and funny that way. Then we ended up sitting together in class. It was engineered under the impatience of our history teacher, who got fed up with Manda's constant giggling and barracking alongside goggle-eyed Stacey Clark on the back row. There was a space by me, with Rebecca Wilson being off poorly, and Manda got shifted.

'Would you sit there and behave, please, Amanda,' Ms. Thompson instructed her, three times, each one louder and a little more desperate.

After tutting in the mardy fashion of a criminal playing victim, she screeched her chair out from under the desk and stalked over to my table. I got to see her eyes up close for the first time, and they were what my Grandad would have called 'ower glisky' – bright after the rain. She looked long at me. I knew it could go either way between us then. When you pen two animals in at short quarters they'll either take to each other and settle into company or they'll set to, gnashing and bucking.

Manda leaned over, clutching her pen tight

and far down its stem, like a little kiddy would hold it, and she drew an inky scribble on the open page of my exercise book. So I put a scrawl back on hers. I did it without pausing – tit for tat. I saw she had a little heart carved into her wrist from a compass point, a thing which only the hailest girls did. The scratch bloomed yellow-red, like a septic rose against her skin. Half way through the lesson her biro ran out and she selected another from my pencil-case without asking. She put it back when she was done.

Something was granted to us afterwards. We were past simply knowing the name of the other and what form we were in. We were allowed to say *Hiya* in passing, in front of our other friends, at the gates of the school, or in Castletown going down to the chippy or the arcade. Not that Manda needed permission for her friendships. She spoke to all manner of folk that were ordinarily off limits to the rest of us: the older, knotty-armed working lads who drove spoilered cars through town on their lunchbreaks and knew her brothers to drink with; the owner and dealers of Toppers nightclub, and the tall, tanned girls who served at the bar there and trod that fine line between being queens and sluts with their reputations for giving good sex, bent over counters after closing time. Inside the old Covered Market, Manda spoke cheekily to the sheepskin-jacketed gents from Carlisle racecourse, as if they were her uncles, and they might have been her uncles.

And there was her mam's lot, the foreign cousins who came to the driving trials from Ireland, Scotland or Mann, and brought with them piebald cobs, fiddles, rumours about filched electronics, litter and un-fettled debts. The town banged on and on about their arrival each year, half of it discrimination, half superstition from a century before. How they were rainmakers and crop-ruiners. How they had curses or the Evil-Eye. How they crossed the Border at night to the peal of the Bowness bells, said to ring out from their wath grave in the Solway when robbers were around, blah blah. Manda stepped into their loud circles and blagged cigarettes and gossiped and got invited to their hakes. She put up with nobody saying within earshot they were dirty potters and pikes.

No grand treaty was needed for her to know me. There came a day when I walked with her and a small crowd downtown for a gravy butty at dinnertime. I was standing near them in the cloakroom waiting for Rebecca to meet me, all of us putting on our coats and ratching in our purses for coins. Her face was dark inside the lum-pool of her hood, and she said,

'Come along on with us if you like, Kathleen.'

'What have you asked her for,' one of the others rasped.

'Because I'm fed up with your ugly mugs,' Manda replied.

She and I walked together with linked arms from the Agricultural Hotel to the bottom of Little Dockray. Who isn't looking at us, I thought, and my heart was going at two-time.

The next month I was one room away while she got laid by a friend of the family – a jockey, who was married with kids. She reported back that he had a prick the size of Scafell and his come had run down her leg. Six weeks after that I sat with her in the clinic while she took two pills for her abortion, and I held her shoulders while she was sick. She said the nurse had told her not to look when she went to the bathroom, but she had looked down into the bucket by her feet. It wasn't like period clots, just a ball of tubes. She said no bloody way was her Mam ever to hear of it because her Mam would've wanted the babby kept.

*

Nine Chimneys was not the house of a rag-and-bone family. The grime of cart-claimed money had been swept back a generation by the Slessors branching out into carpets, property, equestrian prowess. Their travellers' heritage was easily remembered in a town which never forgot former status, but they'd grafted a fortune which made them untouchable by recession, competition, the bitter regional snobbery. The building was low and sprawling. It was almost a mansion except that it looked more like a Yankee ranch, with wooden interiors and a veranda. It had no business being built in Cumbria, one spit off the National Park boundary, and must have been forced past the council planners in the late seventies when the family was in its ascendancy, for it duffed all the local planning laws. There were paddocks front and back of the house for the horses, and slated stables off one wing of the property. Occasionally you could smell the beefy stench of Wildriggs abattoir wafting over from the industrial estate.

Inside there were too many bathrooms to count – I was always scared I'd go in a wrong door – and pungent utility rooms where the Doberman and the Mastiff were kept. There was a sauna and a game room. Everywhere were hung ornately framed pictures of champion breeds, red ribbons indicating the annual royal downfall in the territory, brass reminders of the family sport. There was a long drive up to the house from the Kemplar roundabout and all alongside it were those glistening, hardy ponies, made stout by the gradient of fells, made tame at The Wall by the Romans, and now made fast by the leading reins of the Slessors.

Everybody thought it was Manda's dad who was the horse expert. And with his mule-neck and muscles straining as he bullied them across the beck at Appleby fair, they had no reason not to think it. Geordie was a master of saddlery. He wasn't well respected by the rest of the nation's breeders, the manor house owners and Range-Rover drivers, and that ritted him deeply, but they still came to him for advice and opinion on their steeds, they still bought his stock. He was always interviewed by the regional news-stations after the trophies were won; his yellow Rolls Royce parked prominently behind him. And though he had no right by birth or blood ever to own a car like that, he commanded the cameras in its direction, like it was the golden spoils of a chor shown off by a thief who knew cock to collar he would never get caught.

But it was Vivian Slessor that I saw bringing stubborn geldings into the stables with brobbs of fennel, in the old way of northern handlers. Her crop was seldom used when she rode. Though her racing and rutting knowledge was lesser professionally, as a horse-handler she was somehow greater than Geordie – for her intimacy and charm, her hands working the tender spots behind the creatures' ears to quieten them. Geordie looked to her as his official bonesetter when a horse was damaged, rather than ringing the vet and being billed. He stood back as she bound up a foreleg with sorrel. One windy, mizzling day in April, Vivian Slessor first got me up into the saddle – on a gorgeous chestnut mare too big and blustered for someone of my size and inexperience. She softly talked and tutted as she led us round the paddock in the gale, and I wasn't sure if she was scolding the horse for cross stepping or scolding me for bad posture. At the gap-stead of the field she unclipped the horse's rein.

'Gan on,' she said, and slapped its rump. 'Heels down, Kathleen.'

She was the one who fed the dogs at night and cured illness in the beings under her care. She was like that with her children too. She tended to them without complaint, with a kind of haughty devotion. The old man shouted at the hooligan lads to fucking grit down when they wrestled too near his showcase. He beat them for their cheek and backchat. But Vivian let them tussle and scrap for as long as it took them to thrash it out, until their raised blood got settled. She cleared up after them, wadded lint for the busted noses, collected the smashed plates strewn about the dining room floor. From time to time she stood in court, in her tweed tack-suits and silk scarves, defending an accused son with that pure stare of hers. She had a gannan pride that told the judge he could never undo what she had instilled in her brood, that all the laws of the town, the curfews and fines, the borstal and jail time, mattered not.

But when she did light out towards her own in anger she damaged them badly. Not a one of them ever fought back the way the boys challenged Geordie for supremacy, on and off, if the chance came to them. She could turn loose a blue cruelty, and perhaps they all realised she was capable not least of murder. If she backed up her husband, an argument was immediately lost.

'Get out and sarra them hosses,' he might say to Aaron or Rob, lazy with whisky, from his armchair in the corner.

The lad in question would chunter on about watching the footie match, hating Geordie's cocksure orders. A squabble would loom. Then Vivian Slessor would brush a hand lightly down the back of her son's head and he'd rise up and put on his boots and go to the stables. It was a household of managed tension, and she was at its core. Vivian had a liking for modern things; kitchen appliances, music centres, cars; the sauna was built because she wanted scorching coals without having to go to a public gym. But she was a superstitious woman. Once I saw her take a set of metal tongs from the hearth and beat her eldest across his back for fumbling with her glass Luck. There was some old almanac to her world I didn't understand – belief in plant lore, ritual and sign, maybe some part of it Romany. Come Allhallows she hung dobby stones in the byres to keep the animals safe. She'd put up the roof of her convertible in clear blue skies if there'd been a kessen moon the night before. And she was careful where she'd allow the horse trailers to be parked in a town for the common ridings – never on a gallows hill, which was forbidden, though the horses were allowed to graze there.

I was fascinated to see the parents together. My mother had died when I was eight and my dad never had another woman in his life, so it was an unusual thing, adult intimacy. There was something out of balance in the cottage where I lived, something steeply-slanted. My dad had more heaviness to him than in just his arms and legs and the big belly where he rested his glass after dinner. But he was light compared to my mother's leftovers; her wardrobe of sour-smelling clothes, the elasticated jam-jars and dusty talcums. When I lay in bed at night and heard him grizzling I could feel the building pitch, trying to upend itself, and I'd brace my feet against the bottom of the bed.

The Slessors were even-weighted and indestructible. They'd paired by feral instinct, like wolves among us. If either of them stepped outside the marriage to a different bed – and there were those who gossiped about Geordie's liking for young stable hands, his chance bairns – then it did not threaten the union. They had produced between them three boys and a girl, all fit, all feisty. And there was a sense there might have been more, they had it in them still, he at almost seventy, she at almost fifty. The children bound them, but the two had bindings before, and bindings after. They belonged in the pairing. Even when you saw them singly in the house or around town you knew there must be another half, a mate. Neither went into it for money, for when they began courting there was none. Vivian had owned one dress that would serve for the wedding. All Geordie possessed were a few tons of salvaged pipe and lead shingle.

For all his anger and brash, I never saw him raise a hand to his wife. He could have tried to brutalize her, the way he rode roughshod over everything else in life until it obeyed or broke. But he adored her, this rectifying woman. And he would, in any case, have met his match. He knew it. And moreover she knew it. If the man feared anything, it was his wife's genes, her cuntish atoms. I used to watch as she diced up chicken – the knife would slice and slice, clear of her fingertips, but she'd be watching him as he poured his scotch. Though he'd likely never been near a history book in his life, it was as if Geordie Slessor knew the old region's legacy of women riding alongside men up to the Border, their babies twined across their backs in sacking. She would have taken those fists into her soft flesh, and even worn his black temper on her face in public for a while. Then in the night she would have slit him wide-open, balls to bellybutton. She would've stemmed the blood with secret plant medicine, a draft to make the red come slower, and given him the guttings of his prize colt in exchange for his own liver. Or she'd have granted him something from her domestic realm of keeping the big house; a dinner of ground glass, meat frozen and thawed repeatedly, bannock of foxglove.

She was a handsome woman. Her brow was crosshatched, but lively. Years before she'd had gorgeous tumbling locks, brown and gleaming in their wedding photographs. Perhaps it had thinned or greyed, for she now wore the unwilling bob of a woman proud for most of her life of her hair's beauty, and she'd still sweep it back, invisibly, off her shoulders. Manda got her full chest from her Mam. Vivian was voluptuous, but bone-sculpted at her collar and her jaw. Men opened doors for her. And it was obvious when Geordie wanted her, for he made no game of it, he did not care who witnessed his desire. He'd come at her and grasp her waist. He might even have lifted up her skirts were she not to take it upon herself at these moments to move them both into a private space. Even then their sounds could be heard. After they were done they'd come back into the room easily, unashamed. Everyone knew when they were at it – *Nine Chimneys* took on a different atmosphere. The smell of the horse sweat grew gamier. The boys became edgy and would take to drinking or baiting the dogs. Manda turned up the stereo.

But it was their tender moments that intrigued me most, the brisk expressions of what I took to be love, that would have been mistaken for ordinary occurrences or arguments by anyone not watching them as hard as I watched. Him pulling a spelk out of her hand, pinning her to the table with an elbow and twisting her arm behind her so she couldn't pull away while he doctored her. Him shouting at her from the car window for walking behind a reversing trailer.

'Blind bloody bint!' he spluttered. But it was panic in his voice, not anger.

And I saw her take out her husband's cock and hold it when he came home so drunk from the rugby club that he started to piss himself in the porch of *Nine Chimneys*.

Of the two of them I preferred her, and this surprised me because older women could make me uncomfortable and often I wouldn't know what to talk to them about. But I would have eaten out of her hand without much fuss. Geordie, in a good mood, would flirt with me, and that I could take as acceptance of a kind, mortifying though it was.

'Look at the lass, she's full up, is she not,' he'd say, when Manda and I dressed to go out on a Friday night.

Vivian often said nothing when I was in the room, but she'd sing songs with my name in.

'Maybe I'll go down and see Kathleen,
A swallow comes and tells me of her dreams.
Soon I'm gonna see my sweet Kathleen.'

★

Mostly when we went out it was around town, between the pubs, wherever Manda thought she might catch sight of a lad she was interested in. Sometimes, if one of her brothers didn't mind us coming with him on a delivery or to a gig, we went to the city of Carlisle. It was always a mad trip up, with stupid steering and breakneck over-taking, because the lads loved speed. They loved it on horseback, motorbikes, skis; any vehicle they could make accelerate to flatten their brains against their skulls.

There were two main roads from town – the old toll road, and the Roman, which was nearly disused and cut past the wither of Carrock Fell. And there was the M6. It was a deserted piece of motorway – the last run before Scotland, so it felt like everything was petering out.

I'd sit rammed up against the window, my cheek pressed coldly against it, holding the seatbelt tight across my chest. Manda fought for control of the radio dials while one of her brothers drove. Usually it was Aaron, who would shoot the cambers as if he was on a private racetrack. We crossed that hinterland as people still do now, and they always have done, and they likely always will, regardless of police traps and cameras – moving flat out, at reckless speeds, as if being pursued.

I hated all the passages up to the city; that eerie twenty-five minute slew. Something always seemed to be at our backs along there. This was the original badlands you were taught in school, if you didn't already know. You wouldn't want to linger. You wouldn't want to be caught alone, moving slow and obvious in the lowland. This was where the raiders met, coming south or north. This was burnt-farm, red-river, raping territory. A landscape of torn skirts and hacked throats, where roofs were oiled and fired, and haylofts were used to kipper children. And if you rolled down the window you could just about hear it – the alarms and cackling flames, women split open and screaming as their men-folk choked on sinew pushed down their gullets. The houses in the Borders, if they weren't fortified, were temporary, made of spit and cattle shit and wattle, easy to dismantle, because when the Reivers came you either held fast behind eight hewn feet of rock, or you packed up and ran.

The van leaned hard round chicanes, forcing my cheekbone to the glass, with Aaron singing away to the Roses. Manda seemed fearless on the ride. She seemed to trust the run of things. But I imagined terrible events – wrecks and busted spleens. Adrenalin cleaved my brain wide open, and the giversum old county clambered in. It was said by trainers that up here the gentlest horse could nostril the smoulder of years gone by, taste clinker and burnt skin on the haunted vaults, and it might rear and toss its rider. And for all the Roman straightness, cars would often overturn. There were countless corners where wreaths were laid. Even my dad, normally sedate behind the wheel, leaned hard on the accelerator with his mucky welly through these stretches, not checking the rear-view mirror. He'd fail to indicate when moving lanes; swerve hard as the Land Rover was swiped by gusts from the Pennines. Long-distance drivers, returning home to London and Birmingham, Stafford and Manchester, would often find franked letters from the Cumbrian Police, with points for their license and a hefty fine, and they couldn't quite fathom why they were clocked going over ninety.

Several occasions Aaron Slessor almost killed us driving to Carlisle, and on every one I hated him a bit more. He kept the music loud and ignored us, except for the odd glance at my legs now and then. He went after hares on the tarmac, terrorized other motorists by sitting on their bumper until they moved out of his way. He'd take the back road along the moors, by the Caldew river, brackish as old copper, because it was straight and hummocked and he could try to get all four wheels of the van off the ground. He dropped me home late after each trip, where my dad would be asleep on the sofa with the telly turned low. Aaron didn't complain about ferrying me to and fro, he seemed just to like the drive, the fords and hairpins through the villages. Once or twice he'd ask for a kiss as I was getting out and I'd shove him back and say get lost.

'You're pretty enough to lick out,' he'd say. 'Stop being spooky.'

At nineteen he was the youngest of the Slessor lads, and he'd an almighty chip on his shoulder about that, a desire to be the belted champion in the family. Geordie never got weak enough in his later years not to batter him. If anything he brayed him all the harder – the old family bull recognising his prize fighting days were close to over. That his youngest son took less interest in the horses than the others, while driving the Heltondales tighter on each racecourse's slalom, riled him no end.

'Gudfernobbut twat,' he called his son. 'Runty mutt. You'll amount to fuck all in this life, except laying rugs round fucking bogs.'

Amateur brawlers from the town sought Aaron out, because it was said that to beat him in a fight was to take title over the town. He'd left school not a day after hitching sixteen, and started work at the carpet outlet. He was a looker, with the royal swagger of his old man. I'd seen him go to work on a lass. He had the ability to cut through what little pride she had, to strip her of common sense and condition her to waiting by the phone, waiting outside a pub in the rain, waiting for the characteristic bastard's alba a few weeks later when he'd got bored – telling her she had a dry quim, old biddy skin, fat belly, or spots on her arse and that's why he no longer fancied her.

Nor was he discreet about his conquests. The details of them – the gasps, the games and sexual proclivities – were the chatter of the town for weeks after. How it had been in a horse-trailer and she'd knelt in fresh shit to suck him off. How he'd had her right after her sister in the same evening, a double-dipper. So that his circle of friends had the knowledge of any of his exes they needed before asking them out. And Aaron would occasionally revisit them, Friday nights, if something interested him enough in a bare leg or split-skirt, a new look, a haircut. And they'd let him.

★

It wasn't common that I stayed home. They liked company, the Slessors. They liked having noise and new faces about them. I never felt unwelcome. But the summer after I got to know Manda my father started to notice me being gone. And he said it was a shame, him losing my Mam and now me. The guilt made me hang around for most of the holidays, even though he was out rounding and clipping all day, the house was too chill for the season and it made me fidgety. In the mornings I'd phone up Manda, or she'd phone me.

'Oh bugger Kathleen, can't you come in?' she's say. 'I'm lonely. I'm going to get some new lippy. Fine, alright, ta–rah.'

Then I'd go walking along a scrubby lonning in the village and up the Scar, knowing she'd soon be off into town, having a good time with someone else. From the summit I could see the beacon in the distance, trains dribbling down the mainline, and the ponds of the trout fishery glimmering. On the way home I'd pass by a dilapidated farm, littered with rusting metal-seated tractors, derricks and machinery, tarpaulin strewn about in the yard. The owner of the place was a right bastard, everyone said. He could be heard in the evening yelling obscenities at his dogs and throwing their bowls at them. There'd be howls and yips and yelps. He had any number of hounds and Collies, all rangy and greasy, and half-mad with the frustration you see in workers not put to the flocks.

The farm lay just past a dolt of brambles; I'd pass it after coming through the thorny lane, un-snagging my jeans with a twist of the hips every other step, my arms held overhead. It smelled of Swarfega and slurry, dirt and iron, and something sick, like industry and arable wrongly mixed. The man was known in our village for his bad treatment of animals, though he didn't keep many past the dogs, a handful of bantams, and the occasional pony or scabby penned-in pig. No one reported him to the RSPCA, for doubtless then they'd have to look into their own barns.

But one morning, near the holiday's end, I was walking past the farm's corrugated shed and I noticed the door was open. Usually it was shut and chained, with a thick trestle leaning against it. There was a dead horse lying on the ground between the metal cattle chocks. The ground was slick yellow-brown, like concrete covered in piss and diarrhoea. I stepped closer, in under the gable, and a stink rose.

A shaft of sunlight lit the horse's body. The thing was a mess, shorn of its coat, with sores under its legs and keds crawling all over it. Its ribcage angled up through its flesh like the frame of a boat being dismantled. It had not stood for a long time for its hooves had twisted into thick discoloured spirals, like the nails of a Chinese emperor. For a moment I stood, stupidly looking at the creature. My brain began to flurry. It had not stood for a long time. It had lived on the floor; its hooves not wearing down from grazing and cantering like a properly upright creature. It had lived as it starved.

I took another step in and the horse snorted and moved. It lifted its head and rump together, tamping its torso down on the ground as if meaning to get up, and as it struggled its hooves clicked together and scraped on the floor like flints. It snorted out a pink foam that was lathered in its nostrils, and dragged its back legs again. Click-click. Then it was still.

I cast my eyes around for a pot of water, a blanket, some feed, and saw nothing of any use or comfort. I knew the farmer might be in the bothy, or bent in a shadow nearby, for the shed door would not have been open otherwise, but I couldn't see him. The horse lay unmoving again, as good as gone.

'It's alright, girl,' I whispered, to myself, or to the animal, I wasn't sure which.

Then I walked away. And then I ran.

With every stride, gall rose in me against the man. A dead horse I could have taken. I'd seen much worse – lambs stumbling on the howse, their eyes and arseholes pecked out by the crows, hinds and heads stacked up inside the abattoir. A dead horse was not a problem. But I couldn't stomach a foully living one. My heart harried my blood as I ran. I pulled myself on through the blackthorn, tearing my arms off the burrs without untangling them. My mouth seemed filled with salt and seeds and pellets, though I tried again and again to spit them out along the path.

This farmer had driven one wife to alcohol, Valium, and public breakdowns, and finally a bathtub overdose, it was said. The second had died after falling into the silo. Neglect. Suicide, maybe.

But a patient killing in a reeking shed? No. A wife could up and walk away. She wasn't starved. Her feet weren't bound. This rotted, lying-down horse was worse than anything I'd known. It was something from a middle-forest fairytale, where the dark branches lift and in a clearing is Knife-Hand-Nick, his children's heads bubbling in a pot above the fire. It was like meeting Nelly Wood in your dreams, when she stitches your skin to the hem of her cloak and flies away, dragging your pelt behind her, so in the morning you wake up flayed.

I stopped in the briar and leant over and was sick.

By the time I got back to the village I was patch-worked with bramble gashes, and blood was dripping off my elbows. In my head I could still hear the skeltering hooves, scraping and clicking and scraping on the ground. I thought I'd go to the top field and tell my dad to fetch the vet. I thought I'd go into the house, take the shotgun from its rack above the mantle and kill the horse myself, or kill the man, or kill them both. But, like a reprieve, the blue Slessor van was parked outside the Fox and Pheasant, by the village green, and I saw Aaron climbing back inside from a delivery, or a pint, whatever reason he'd been there. He rolled the window down as I walked up.

'Now then, Kathleen. What have you done

to yourself, you daft tuss?' he asked, looking me over.

'Nothing. Just come with me will you,' I said, and he laughed.

'Aye, aye.'

'It's not a joke, Aaron. Come with me now. Please. I really want you to.'

He tucked his bottom lip under his teeth and had me stand there against the blue bore of his eyes. Then he opened the door and climbed down out of the van. Maybe he came for curiosity about the blood on my arms, already drying in black gobs from the summer heat. Or for the chance his sister's friend would let him move her knickers to one side, like he'd been after for weeks. Or maybe it was my tone, the bite of it, for I'd never spoken so assuredly to him before. Any other day I'd have been ignored, or he'd have flustered me with a tease. But he followed me through the ginnel, calling me a dippy bint, complaining he'd torn his shirt on the briar, and saying it better be worth it.

When we got to the corrugated shed the door was closed up and trestle-jammed again.

'Give us a hand shifting this.'

'Dirty little spot you've got in mind,' he said. 'You're a surprise, girly.'

I was shaking as we moved the timber, and breathing hard. He must have thought I'd become a lunatic, some lusty version of the girl he'd seen knocking about his house so many times. When I pulled the metal latch off its snick he put his hand on my back and gripped my vest into a ball of cloth, un-tucking it from my jeans. He stepped in close behind me and held my hips.

I pulled opened the door. The sun had moved over a bit and it was dark inside, all spooled with shadow. The smell was throaty and rank, like something from a tannery, or a dog pound before the cages are hosed.

'There,' I said, 'can you see it?'

'Oh, in a minute you know I will.'

He pulled me back harder against him, one arm belted across my stomach, one hand at the zip of my jeans. There was a pause. In my ear I heard a grating sound, like a piece of machinery slipping its driving gear. Aaron let go. He stepped round in front of me. Then he turned and drove me backwards out of the building, his palm splayed on my breastbone, pressing my nipple in painfully. I tripped on the concrete slab behind and went down.

'Fuck off.'

I looked up and he was standing above, his face in a twist, looking kiltered as if to hit me.

'Fuck off home, Kathleen. It's not your business, this. It's not your concern.'

'Get. The fuck. Away,' he said. 'Go on! Now!' His bicep jumped.

I stood and stumbled off, thinking myself so

horribly soft-minded, and only then did I feel my eyes begin to speckle and sting. I waited for him inside our cottage, with my cheek on the cold larder wall. I waited. But he didn't come. When I looked out of the upstairs window the carpet van had gone.

The next week I heard nothing at all from Manda. When I phoned the house Vivian said she was out and she said it in a tone that made me not inclined to ask anything else. Manda never phoned back. I stayed indoors. When I walked it was in the other direction to the farm.

The summer went on, and then it ended. By then I was sure they all must have taken against me for what had happened, for my babyish behaviour, and that was my worst fear. I thought about those times Manda had fought someone; the wet sound of knuckles against cartilage; the rows of double stitches required above her victim's eyebrows after she was done.

I took the first few days of the new term off sick, though I had no fever and my dad suspected it. Then I worried this would make it worse. I imagined Sharon Kitchen and Stacey Clark huddled round Manda before registration like rooks on their desks, cawing in her ear that I was always a too-clever bitch, or they'd heard I'd called her a slag, and she should pull me down a peg or two. I knew all some girls needed as an excuse to start hating you was your absence, your lack of defence.

On my first day back she came to find me in the cloakroom. She stood next to me, the old group hovering by the door. I kept my eyes down. I heard her say my name. Then I felt her fingers digging in under my ribs to make me squirm.

'No you don't,' she said as I twitched away. 'Where've you been, you silly cow? Off shagging some mucky farmer?'

When I looked at her she had a big smirk going. I knew she was pleased to see me.

'Right. Come on,' she said, putting her arm round my shoulders. 'Think we better have a quiet word – it's been pande-bloody-monium. Get lost the rest of you. Ah, shit it, there's the bell! Meet you at twelve.'

That lunchtime, in the bandstand in the park, Manda told me what had happened. Aaron had rung up their brothers from the Pheasant, and they'd come, because they always did come when it was put to them they had a duty. They'd searched the vicinity for the ratchety farmer – Malcolm Miller was his name. She said the lads knew the fellow marginally anyway from the cockfights in the pits near Greystoke, and he was a sly git, so it was no trouble to them. They'd strung him up in the shed by his feet and cut the bastard with a riding crop right through to the putty in his spine. He was in Newcastle Infirmary, she said, not expected to walk again.

I searched her face for some sign of

disturbance, and saw nothing favourable. Her eyes were that glisky blue, all bad charm and cheek.

'I thought you already knew,' she said. 'Thought you were just being canny and swinging wide. We've had the police up at the house about a million times. But it's just his word.'

Manda took my arm as she always did. We walked through the park gates down into town, past the sandstone terraces and castle tower. She talked about the parties I'd missed that summer, the fairs and driving trials, and asked if I'd had any lads properly yet.

'No,' I said.

'Well, what you bloody waiting for? Or do you want Aaron to do the deed. Urgh.'

As we walked I thought about the man, lying lame in a hospital bed.

'What about the horse?' I asked.

Manda shrugged. Her attention was on the construction site across the road. A builder in a red checked shirt whistled from the scaffolding. She blew him a kiss.

I knew if it'd been any other animal inside that barn, the Slessors would not have intervened. They wouldn't have done it for the kicked-about hounds. And they didn't do it for me. There was nothing sentimental to the family, nor could they be hired like mercenaries. It was simply the family's creed. It was luck, if such a thing could be so called. To slow-butcher a horse was an offence great enough it could not pass. Their spurs were buckled on and used accordingly.

'Mam says you've to come for your tea next week,' Manda said to me as we headed back up to school. 'The hornies will have gone by then and she'll take you riding. She's got a new pony for you. And you'll never guess what she's called it. Sweet Kathleen.'

If It Keeps On Raining

Jon McGregor

THIS IS HOW his days begin. If you really want to know. Standing in his doorway in the cold wet morning light and pissing on the stony ground. Waking up and getting out of bed and walking across the rough wooden floor. Opening the door and pulling down the front of his pyjama trousers and the weight of a whole night's piss pouring out onto the stony ground and winding down to the river which flows out to the sea. The relief of it. The long sighing relief of it. He has to hold on to the door-frame to keep his balance, he says.

He looks at the swirl and churn of the river. Boats passing, driftwood and debris. A drowned animal turning slowly in the current. The people in the boats wave, sometimes, but he doesn't wave back. He didn't ask them to come sweeping past like that while he's having his morning piss. In their shining white boats with the chrome guard-rails and the tinted windows and the little swim-decks on the stern. As if they'd ever swim in this river. They can come past if they like but they shouldn't expect him to wave. Not when his hands are full.

Sometimes there's a man on the other side of the river, fishing. It's too far to see his face, so it's hard to tell whether the man can see what he's doing. But if he could he wouldn't be embarrassed. This is his house now, and there's nothing to stop him pissing on his own ground when he wakes up each day.

They come past mainly in the summer months, the boats, but the man fishing is there all year round. He brings a lot of accessories with him. He's got two or three different rods, and rests to set them in, and a big metal case that he sits on with all sorts of trays and drawers and compartments, and he keeps getting up to open all the drawers and trays one after the other. As if he's looking for something. As if he hasn't got any kind of an ordered storage system. He's got this one net, like a long tube closed off at one end, he has it trailing in the water with the open end pegged down on the bank. He uses it to keep the fish in when he catches them. It's not clear why. Maybe he likes to count them at the end of the day. Or maybe he likes the way they look when he empties them back into the river, the silver flashes of them pouring through the air like electricity, the way they wriggle and flap for a second as though they were trying to fly. Or maybe he likes the company.

And he's got this other net, a big square net on the end of a long pole. It's not clear but it looks like if he gets fed up with all the rods and reels and maggots and not being able to find what he's looking for in those drawers he could just sit on the edge of the bank and sweep it through the river until he comes up with something. Like a child at the seaside. Like a little boy with one of those coloured nets on the end of a bamboo cane.

Like a little boy whose dad was showing him how to use one of those nets, and he lost it. At the seaside. When they were out on a jetty, and he was sweeping the net back and forth through the clear salt-water, and the boy was pulling at his arm to say: Let me try let me have a go, and the man dropped it in the water somehow. Just let it slip out of his hand, and it floated out on the swell of a wave and sank. The little boy wanted him to jump in and get it, and his father had to say: I'm sorry I can't. And the little boy wanted him to buy another one and the man had to say, again: I'm sorry I can't. The boy started crying and there wasn't much the man could do about it. He could have picked him up.

The way these things pop into his head sometimes. Standing there in the morning, looking at someone fishing, pissing on the stony ground that slopes down to the river, thinking about nothing much and then a man losing his little boy's net pops into his head from years back. This really was some years back now. The way he couldn't buy a new net to make it better. The little boy with a mess of pale red hair.

He stands there each morning and he looks at the river, the fields, the sky. He tries to estimate what the weather will do for the rest of the day. He makes some decisions about the work he's going to do on the treehouse or the raft. He thinks about making some breakfast. He thinks about going out to look for some wood.

It's hard to understand why the people on the boats always wave. Perhaps they feel strange being out in the middle of the water like that. They feel vulnerable or lonely and it helps if they wave, maybe. Or maybe they think it's just what they're supposed to do. Maybe they say Ahoy when they pass another boat. Who knows. The men on the commercial boats never wave. There's one that goes by about once a week, and he's never seen them waving the whole time he's been here, not at him or the man fishing or at any of the other boats. It's a sand-barge or a gravel-barge or something like that. When it goes upstream it sits high on the water, its tall panelled sides beaten like a steel drum. But coming back down, fully loaded with sand or gravel or whatever, it looks like a different boat, sunk low in the water, steady and stately and slow, a man in a flat blue cap walking the wave-lapped gunwales and washing them down with a long-handled mop he dips in the churning water. And he wonders, often, what would happen if the man slipped and fell in, if he would prove to be a good swimmer, if the driver of the boat would be able to stop and pull him back on board. Or if the man would drown and wash ashore, if perhaps he would come flopping limply onto the bank where this small piece of stony land slopes down to the water.

He's not sure what he would do if that were to happen. He doesn't know if he would be able to step down towards the man then, and pick him up. Or at least grab hold of him and drag him clear of the river. He's not sure if he'd be able to do it. Physically. Mentally. Maybe the right thing would be to wait for the proper authorities to arrive. Maybe his part could be to walk out along the road to the phone-box by the yacht club and do the necessary informing. They might come along and say: Thank you sir, you did the right thing. It was the right thing not to touch the body, well done. And they'd take photos, of the stony ground, the body, the feet still paddling in the edge of the river. And people with the appropriate experience and accessories would come and pick him up, out of the water, and take him away.

They'd need the right accessories.

The other man on the boat, the driver or the skipper or whatever, he wouldn't be able to do much to help. It's a big boat, a really big boat, he wouldn't be able to just stop and pull over like after a car accident, he couldn't just steer over to the bank and moor up and come running over shouting: Where is he, where is he, is he ok? It wouldn't be like that. He would have to continue his passage, steer the boat on to its destination or if he was lucky to an available mooring pontoon which might be closer, and he would have to moor the boat properly, by himself, and then come back to this location. And it's possible that by then the proper authorities would have been and gone, and taken his mop-dangling friend with them.

He imagines the skipper at the wheel of his heavy-laden barge, looking back at the spot in the river where his friend had slipped in. It would be difficult. Two men doing a job like that, every day, they could become very close. They could develop a close understanding of each other. Up and down the same stretch, loading and unloading, tying and untying, not saying much to each other because the noise of the engine would make it difficult to hear and because anyway what would there be to say. But understanding each other with a look and a nod, and a way of standing or a way of holding themselves, they could become very close, they would know each other better than perhaps they know anyone else. And then one of them slips from the wet gunwale into the water and his friend can only turn and look, the water closing over him as if nothing had happened and the long-handled mop floating out to sea.

He thinks about this a lot, he says. But, who knows. It doesn't seem worth dwelling on. It seems an unlikely thing to need to consider, the proper procedure in such an event. But it's not an entirely unlikely occurrence. It happens. It has happened. People fall in the water, and they disappear, and they reappear drowned. It's not unlikely. It's a thing that can happen.

Perhaps that's why they don't wave, the men on the barges, because they're concentrating, because they know about the things that can happen, because they take the river seriously.

He watches them, when they pass, the man in the flat blue cap with the mop and the man at the wheel, and he wonders if they see him. If they see the man fishing, when he's there, which is quite often, or if they see anything besides the river and the current and the weather and each other.

He imagines they keep quite a close watch on the weather, the two of them. We've always got half an eye on it, they'd probably say, if someone asked them, if they came into the yacht club one evening and someone bought them a drink and talked to them about working that great boat up and down the river. It has quite an effect on our operation.

He keeps a close watch on the weather as well, from his place on the riverbank. It changes quite slowly. He can see it happening way over in the distance, a turn in the wind, a break in the clouds, a veil of rain rolling in across the fields. Sometimes he thinks it would be interesting to keep a chart of it, windspeeds and temperatures and total rainfall. That type of thing. But it would need certain equipment, certain know-how and measuring equipment and he's not sure where someone would come by that type of thing. Probably it would mean going into town.

But sometimes it can really take his breath away, he says, how different this place can look, with a change in the weather. He can stand in the doorway sometimes, first thing in the morning and all the rain from the day before has vanished and there are no clouds and it looks like maybe there never were any clouds and there never will be again, the sky is that clear and clean and huge, and everything that was grey before is fresh and bright like newly-sawn wood. And then other times he can stand here and see nothing, the thick mist lifting up off the river and nothing visible besides the trees around his house. The river just a muffled sound of water rushing over the stony banks. The opposite bank completely lost, and no clue as to whether the fisherman is there or not with his rods and his nets and his accessories box. The fisherman doesn't seem the sort to let a damp day put him off his fishing, but there's no way of knowing.

It's frustrating, he says, not being able to know. He's a man who likes to know these things. What's happening in his immediate surroundings. The lie of the land. Sometimes he's even thought about walking round to the man's spot to find out, to make sure. But it's a long walk, and there are things he has to do with his time. It would be about six miles altogether, out along the road past the yacht club, into the village, past the post office, out by the farm to the new road bridge and across and then all the way back along the other bank.

And what would he say to him when he got there anyway. It would be awkward.

People call it the new road bridge, but it must be twenty or thirty years old.

It's not just the weather that changes. It's surprising, how new a day can look, how different the view can be when he stands there each morning having a piss on the stony ground. The height of the water, the colour of the sky, the feel of the air against his skin, the direction of the smoke drifting out from the cooling towers along the horizon, the number of leaves on the trees, the footprints of birds and small animals in the soft mud at the water's edge, the colour and noise and speed of the river running by.

He asked me to tell you these things.

The speed of the water changes, that's something else, with the height of the river. If it's been raining a lot. The river draws itself up, the water churning brown with all the mud washed in off the fields and the water rises up and races towards the sea, sweeping round bends and rushing over rocks or trees or sunken boats that sit and rest in its way, anything that thinks it can just rest where it is, the river rushes over it and sooner or later picks it up and carries it along, like loose soil and stones on the banks of outside bends, or trees with fragile roots, or a stack of pallets left too close to the water's edge, it all gets swept along like small children in a crowd, like what happens in a football ground if there are too many people in not enough space and something happens to make everyone rush, if they all start to run and then no one person can stop or avoid it, they all move together and then what do you expect if you try and put a dam against all that momentum, if you put up a fence and say stand back don't run there's enough room for everyone if you spread out and stand back and stop pushing.

When there's not enough room. When there's too many of them and someone puts up a fence and says stop pushing.

That's what it's like, he says. The river. When it's been raining too much. The momentum of it is huge and dangerous: it makes him think of a crowd of people being swept along and none of them can stop it and they get to a fence and someone says stop pushing. In a football ground. Everybody rushing into one space and there's not enough room and no-one can stop moving. And there's a fence and someone standing behind the fence says: Stop pushing will you all please stop pushing.

It's what comes to mind, when he sees the river like that.

And other times the river is quiet, almost timid. Sometimes, after a few days of the river raging past all choked with mud and fury, after the rain has stopped, it drops back down again, slows, slips away from the high carved banks and comes to what looks like a standstill. The sun in broken shards across its surface, as if scraps of tinfoil had been thrown in from a bridge by some children further upstream. It looks good enough to swim in, then. Not that he ever has. He's never seen anyone swimming here. It doesn't seem like a good idea.

*

So. This is how his days begin. If you wanted to know. The morning creeps through the cracked and taped windows of his house. He stands in the doorway, pissing on the stony ground, and he thinks about all these things. He looks at the river, and the sky, and the weather, and he thinks about his work for the day. He tries to allocate his priorities. The treehouse is almost finished, apart from the roof, but the raft is still a long way from being done.

The roof will be important.

He thinks about the people on the boats, and the man fishing, and children further upstream throwing things into the water. Throwing sticks and model boats, pieces of paper rolled up and jammed into plastic bottles with screw-top lids. He imagines the bottles rolling up on to his piece of land, by chance, and he imagines unscrewing the lids and unrolling the pieces of paper. He thinks about the children, on the bridge, watching the model boats and the plastic bottles turning in the current. He imagines them shielding their eyes to catch a last glimpse. Two of them, a boy and a girl, the girl almost eleven now, the boy eight and a half. Red-haired, like their father. He imagines the girl turning away and saying: Come on, we should catch up with Mum now, and the boy saying: But I can still see mine, I can. Holding his small hands up to his eyes like binoculars.

And what would he read, on the pieces of paper?

The sky looks clear right across to the far field; clear and soft and blue, a faint early sun shining off the river. But there's a cold wind, and there's rain on the way.

Yellowed willow leaves blow across the stony ground and into the river, floating away like tiny boats heading out to sea.

And when it starts. They won't understand. They'll put on coats and go outside, brandishing umbrellas against the violence of the sky. They'll check the forecast and wait for the rain to stop so they can hang the washing outside. But it won't stop. They should understand, but they won't.

The treehouse is almost done. It was slow when he started; he didn't really know what he was doing.

He had to try a few different techniques before he could progress. There was less urgency then. There's more now. It's sort of imperative that he gets it finished soon. He's used pallets mostly. They're easy to get hold of, and if it looks a bit untidy then so what. At least it does the job.

Some of the others in the yacht club have noticed. They must have seen it from the road when they were driving past. They were laughing about it last time he went in. One of them asked if his name was Robinson and where was the rest of the Swiss family, and he almost did something then, like swinging a big glass ashtray into the side of his head or pushing him off his stool. But he didn't. He's more careful now. Accidents and things like that happen very easily, if he's not careful. So he didn't say a thing. They asked him lots of questions, like what was he building it for and why was it so high and what was he going to do when the winds picked up. He just said he had some wood lying around and he thought he'd give it a go, and when someone beat their chest and made a noise like Tarzan he got up and left. He didn't even slam the door, and he didn't go back when he heard them laugh.

Who knows why they call it the yacht club. None of them have got yachts.

The way they laughed. Some people deserve it, what will come. What will fall.

It might not be the finest treehouse ever built, but it does what it needs to do. It's difficult to get the details exactly right, fifty foot in the air and the shadow of rain clouds looming overhead. It's hard enough getting every last piece of wood up there in the first place, climbing up and down to fasten the ropes and hauling it hand over hand. It would be easier with two people. Or quicker, at least. But it's just him, now, so it takes some careful planning. Some forethought. And hard work.

He just needs some roofing felt, that's all. Or an old tarpaulin, if he can't find any felt. The roof will be important. He'll need to take his time over the roof. And then there's the raft, of course. He's got the basic structure, the barrels and the pallets. But it needs more work on the lashings. It's the structural integrity which will count, in the long run. It might need some kind of shelter as well, a little cabin or a frame for a tarpaulin. If it can take the weight.

The weather, when it changes, it generally comes rolling in from the east, from over by the new road bridge. He can stand here and watch the clouds gathering, like an army forming up on a distant hillside and preparing to march. Only when it comes in it's more of a charge than a march, crashing into the river, and a noise like boxes of nails spilling on to a wooden floor. When it comes like that, furious and sudden, it usually passes by again soon enough, the air beaten clean in its wake.

But there will come a time when it doesn't pass. When the clouds gather and don't pass away, and rain pours endlessly upon the Earth. And some will be prepared, and some will not.

He wonders what the man on the other side of the river does, when he's not here. When he's not fishing. Probably he's retired and that's why he can manage to be here so often. But he doesn't look old enough to be retired, the way he walks, the weight he carries. Maybe he got grounds of ill health out of someone, out of whoever he was working for. The police, maybe, it's quite possible to get grounds of ill health with the police, like mental distress or something, like if something were to happen, there are things that can happen if you work in the police, there are things that can give you stress or mental distress. For example things you might witness or be a part of.

Like being in front of a crowd, and saying: Stop pushing there's enough room for everyone there's no need to push. Like being the other side of a fence and saying: Get back stop pushing. And later you see the rails, steel rails, bent and broken as easily as reeds.

It could be difficult for someone to do their job, after that, to carry that with them and not be affected by the mental distress. Fishing might be ideal after that, the order and routine of it, the quietness, the solitude. No-one shouting. No-one pushing. No-one asking for explanations. Just the river, easing on past. The sky, the changing light, the flash of silver from the emptying net when the fish pour back into the river's swirl and churn.

It might not be that, of course. That would just be speculation. It might be nothing like that at all.

When it comes it will come suddenly, rushing across the Earth like a vengeful crowd, an unturnable tide of seething fury. This: he knows this. They will stand and watch, in bus-shelters, in shop doorways, from the apparent safety of locked cars, and they will say: Oh, isn't the weather awful, tutting, and they will not know what they say.

And perhaps two children on a bridge, throwing scraps of paper into the water, watching the water rise higher and higher, perhaps they will have the sense to know what is happening, perhaps they will climb a tree and scan the horizon for a place of safety. Or perhaps in desperation they will take their umbrellas and turn them into boats, drop them into the water and ride the upturned parasols wherever the current carries them. Or perhaps they're too big for that now.

And whenever it looks as though the rain will stop, people will come out of their houses and peer up at the sky. They will lift their faces and let themselves be soaked while they stare at the thinning clouds, retreating to the safety of their houses, their upstairs bedrooms, their rooftops.

This will be in the first few weeks. Before they realise.

When it happens there will be people rushing by, the torrential current of the new river sweeping them quickly and terribly past. And he won't be able to help them. But he'll look, and if he sees two little ones hurtling along, two red-haired wide-eyed little ones, he'll reach out with a big net on the end of a long pole he's got there ready, and he'll pull them in, dry them off and wrap them up warm and cook them supper. And they can all stay together in the treehouse for as long as it takes, and if the children get bored there will be paper and crayons for them to draw with, write messages on, make little model boats. And if they need to leave they'll have the raft. They'll be ready.

The sky is clear now, but the rain is coming. He can smell it.

Sometimes when he wakes it's still only just

getting light. It's good, to stand there and watch the morning creep up on the world, the river a shadow in front of him, the cold air against his skin. It's a privilege. Sometimes he can just stand there for a whole hour, watching the shapes and colours taking form out of the darkness. The streams and ditches all glinting like silver threads.

It is sometimes a very beautiful world. It's a shame, what will happen.

It's rare though, to spend an hour watching the morning arrive like that. People don't. It's rare for people to even spend a moment enjoying their first piss of the day, the way he does. People are so busy. They'll brush their teeth sitting on the toilet to save a few minutes. Eat breakfast standing up. They don't have the time to watch the colour bleed into the world each day. They have meetings, schedules, documents. They don't have time to listen to each other, to be patient with the difficulties of expression. They haven't got the time to stand and watch a man say nothing except: I can't explain, or: I don't know how to say it. There are important things to be done, and a man who will spend a day standing at a window is not a man who can fit into such functional and fulfilling lives.

These are not people with ears to hear or eyes to

see. These are not people who will understand, when it comes.

They will say they understand. They will say they know it might take a while to come to terms. But one day there will be shouting, there will be a cracked voice saying: I don't have time to deal with all this. There will be the banging of objects against hard surfaces, a waving of arms, children standing and crying.

They don't have time. They have busy and important things to do. They need somebody who can be there for them. They need somebody who can go back to work, even after that. Silence and stillness and contemplation aren't going to pay the bills.

This is how his days begin, now. He asked me to tell you. He wakes up, he walks across the rough wooden floor, he holds on to the doorframe and he pisses onto the stony ground.

He looks at the height of the river and the colour of the sky. He looks up at the half-built treehouse, and the raft, and he plans his work for the day.

Soon it will rain. And people won't understand. They'll just put on their hats and coats, open their umbrellas, and rush out into the middle of whatever it is they need to do. Their busy days. Their successful and important lives.

He thought you should know.

My Daughter the Racist

Helen Oyeyemi

ONE MORNING MY daughter woke up and said all in a rush: 'Mother, I swear before you and God that from today onwards I am racist.' She's eight years old. She chopped all her hair off two months ago because she wanted to go around with the local boys and they wouldn't have her with her long hair. Now she looks like one of them; eyes dazed from looking directly at the sun, teeth shining white in her sunburnt face. She laughs a lot. She plays. 'Look at her playing,' my mother says. 'Playing in the rubble of what used to be our great country.' My mother exaggerates as often as she can. I'm sure she would like nothing more than to be part of a Greek tragedy. She wouldn't even want a large part, she'd be perfectly content with a chorus role, warning that fate is coming to make havoc of all things. My mother is a fine woman, all over wrinkles and she always has a clean handkerchief somewhere about her person, but I don't know what she's talking about with her rubble this, rubble that — we live in a village, and it's not bad here. Not peaceful, but not bad. In cities it's worse. In the city centre, where we used to live, a bomb took my husband and turned his face to blood. I was lucky, another widow told me, that there was something left so that I could know of his passing. But I was ungrateful. I spat at that widow. I spat at her in her sorrow. That's sin. I know that's sin. But half my life was gone, and it wasn't easy to look at what was left.

Anyway, the village. I live with my husband's mother, whom I now call my mother, because I can't return to the one who gave birth to me. It isn't done. I belong with my husband's mother until someone else claims me. And that will never happen, because I don't wish it.

The village is hushed. People observe the phases of the moon. In the city I felt the moon but hardly ever remembered to look for it. The only thing that disturbs us here in the village is the foreign soldiers. Soldiers, soldiers, soldiers, patrolling. They fight us and they try to tell us, in our own language, that they're freeing us. Maybe, maybe not. I look through the dusty window (I can never get it clean, the desert is our neighbour) and I see soldiers every day. They think someone dangerous is running secret messages through here; that's what I've heard. What worries me more is the young people of the village. They stand and watch the soldiers. And the soldiers don't like it, and the soldiers point their guns, especially at the young men. They won't bother with the women and girls, unless the woman or the girl has an especially wild look in her eyes. I think there are two reasons the soldiers don't like the young men watching them. The first reason is that the soldiers know they are ugly in their boots and fatigues, they are perfectly aware that their presence spoils everything around them. The second reason is the nature of the watching – the boys and the men around here watch with a very great hatred, so great that it feels as if action must follow. I feel that sometimes, just walking past them – when I block their view of the soldiers these boys quiver with impatience.

And that girl of mine has really begun to stare at the soldiers, too, even though I slap her hard when I catch her doing that. Who knows what's going to happen? These soldiers are scared. They might shoot someone. Noura next door says: 'If they could be so evil as to shoot children then it's in God's hands. Anyway I don't believe that they could do it.'

But I know that such things can be. My husband was a university professor. He spoke several languages, and he gave me books to read, and he read news from other countries and told me what's possible. He should've been afraid of the world, should've stayed inside with the doors locked and the blinds drawn, but he didn't do that, he went out. Our daughter is just like him. She is part of his immortality. I told him, when I was still carrying her, that that's what I want, that that's how I love him. I had always dreaded and feared pregnancy, for all the usual reasons that girls who daydream more than they live fear pregnancy. My body, with its pain and mess and hunger – if I could have bribed it to go away, I would have. Then I married my man, and I held fast to him. And my brain, the brain that had told me I would never bear a child for any man, no matter how nice he was, that brain began to tell me something else. Provided the world continues to exist, provided conditions remain favourable, or at least tolerable, our child will have a child and that child will have a child and so on, and with all those children of children come the inevitability that glimpses of my husband will resurface, in their features, in the way they use their bodies, a fearless swinging of the arms as they walk. Centuries from now some quality of a man's gaze, smile, voice, way of standing or sitting will please someone else in a way that they aren't completely aware of, will be loved very hard for just a moment, without enquiry into where it came from. I ignore the women who say that my daughter does things that a girl shouldn't do, and when I want to keep her near me, I let her go. But not too far, I don't let her go too far from me.

The soldiers remind me of boys from here sometimes. The way our boys used to be. Especially when you catch them with their helmets off, three or four of them sitting on a wall at lunchtime, trying to enjoy their sandwiches and the sun, but really too restless for both. Then you see the rifles beside their lunchboxes and you remember that they aren't our boys.

'Mother… did you hear me? I said that I am now a racist.'

I was getting my daughter ready for school. She can't tie knots but she loves her shoelaces to make extravagant bows.

'Racist against whom, my daughter?'

'Racist against soldiers.'

'Soldiers aren't a race.'

'Soldiers aren't a race,' she mimicked. 'Soldiers aren't a race.'

'What do you want me to say?'

She didn't have an answer, so she just went off in a big gang with her schoolfriends. And I worried, because my daughter has always seen soldiers – in her lifetime she hasn't known a time or place when the cedars stood against the blue sky without khaki canvas or crackling radio signals in the way.

An hour or so later Bilal came to visit. A great honour, I'm sure, a visit from that troublesome Bilal who had done nothing but pester me since the day I came to this village. He sat down with us and mother served him tea.

'Three times I have asked this daughter of yours to be my wife,' Bilal said to my mother. He shook a finger at her. As for me, it was as if I wasn't there. 'First wife,' he continued. 'Not even second or third – first wife.'

'Don't be angry, son,' my mother murmured. 'She's not ready. Only a shameless woman could be ready so soon after what happened.'

'True, true,' Bilal agreed. A fly landed just above my top lip and I let it walk.

'Rather than ask a fourth time I will kidnap her…'

'Ah, don't do that, son. Don't take the light of an old woman's eyes,' my mother murmured, and she fed him honey cake. Bilal laughed from his belly, and the fly fled. 'I was only joking.'

The third time Bilal asked my mother for my hand in marriage I thought I was going to have to do it after all. But my daughter said I wasn't allowed. I asked her why. Because his face is fat and his eyes are tiny? Because he chews with his mouth open?

'He has a tyrannical moustache,' my daughter said. 'It would be impossible to live with.' I'm proud of her vocabulary. But it's starting to look as if I think I'm too good for Bilal, who owns more cattle than any other man for miles around and could give my mother, daughter and I everything we might reasonably expect from this life.

Please, God. You know I don't seek worldly things. If you want me to marry again, so be it. But please – not Bilal. After the love that I have had... you don't believe me, but I would shatter.

My daughter came home for her lunch. After prayers we shared some cold karkedeh, two straws in a drinking glass, and she told me what she was learning, which wasn't much. My mother was there, too, rattling her prayer beads and listening indulgently. She made faces when she thought my daughter talked too much. Then we heard the soldiers coming past as usual, and we went and looked at them through the window. I thought we'd make fun of them a bit, as usual. But my daughter ran out of the front door and into the path of the army truck, yelling: 'You! You bloody soldiers!' Luckily the truck's wheels crawled along the road, and the body of the truck itself was slumped on one side, resigned to a myriad of pot holes. Still, it was a very big truck, and my daughter is a very small girl.

I was out after her before I knew what I was doing, shouting her name. It's a good name – we chose a name that would grow with her, but she seemed determined not to make it to adulthood. I tried to trip her up, but she was too nimble for me. Everyone around was looking on from windows and the open gates of courtyards. The truck rolled to a stop. Someone inside it yelled: 'Move, kid. We've got stuff to do.'

I tried to pull my daughter out of the way, but she wasn't having any of it. My hands being empty, I wrung them. My daughter began to pelt the soldier's vehicle with stones from her pockets. Her pockets were very deep that afternoon, her arms lashed the air like whips. Stone after stone bounced off metal and rattled glass, and I grabbed at her and she screamed: 'This is my country! Get out of here!'

The people of the village began to applaud her. 'Yes,' they cried out, from their seats in the audience, and they clapped. I tried again to seize her arm and failed again. The truck's engine revved up and I opened my arms as wide as they would go, inviting everyone to witness. Now I was screaming too: 'So you dare? You really dare?'

And there we were, mother and daughter, causing problems for the soldiers together.

Finally a scrawny soldier came out of the vehicle without his gun. He was the scrawniest fighting man I've ever seen – he was barely there, just a piece of wire, really. He walked towards my daughter, who had run out of stones. He stretched out a long arm, offering her chewing gum, and she swore at him, and I swore at her for swearing. He stopped about thirty centimetres away from us and said to my daughter: 'You're brave.'

My daughter put her hands on her hips and glared up at him.

'We're leaving tomorrow,' the scrawny soldier told her.

Whispers and shouts: *the soldiers are leaving tomorrow!*

A soldier inside the truck yelled out: 'Yeah, but more are coming to take our place,' and everyone piped low. My daughter reached for a stone that hadn't fallen far. Who is this girl? Four feet tall and fighting something she knows nothing about. Even if I explained it to her she wouldn't get it. I don't get it myself.

'Can I shake your hand?' the scrawny soldier asked her, before her hand met the stone. I thought my girl would refuse, but she said yes. 'You're okay,' she told him. 'You came out to face me.'

'Her English is good,' the coward from within the truck remarked.

'I speak to her in English every day,' I called out. 'So she can tell people like you what she thinks.'

We stepped aside then, my daughter and I, and let them continue their patrol.

★

My mother didn't like what had happened. But didn't you see everyone clapping for us, my daughter asked. So what, my mother said. People clap at anything. Some people even clap when they're on an aeroplane and it lands. That was something my husband had told us from his travels – I hadn't thought she'd remember.

My daughter became a celebrity amongst the children, and from what I saw, she used it for good, bringing the shunned ones into the inner circle and laughing at all their jokes.

★

The following week a foreigner dressed like one of our men knocked at my mother's door. It was late afternoon, turning to dusk. People sat looking out onto the street, talking about everything as they took their tea. Our people really know how to discuss a matter from head to toe; it is our gift, and such conversation on a balmy evening can be sweeter than sugar. Now they were talking about the foreigner who was at our door. I answered it myself. My daughter was at my side and we recognized the man at once; it was the scrawny soldier. He looked itchy and uncomfortable in his djellaba, and he wasn't wearing his keffiyeh at all correctly – his hair was showing.

'What a clown,' my daughter said, and from her seat on the cushioned floor my mother vowed that clown, or no clown, he couldn't enter her house.

'Welcome,' I said to him. It was all I could think of to say. See a guest, bid him welcome. It's who we are. Or maybe it's just who I am.

'I'm not here to cause trouble,' the scrawny soldier said. He was looking to the north, south, east and west so quickly and repeatedly that for some seconds his head was just a blur. 'I'm completely off duty. In fact, I've been on leave since last week. I'm just – I just thought I'd stick around for a little while. I thought I might have met a worthy adversary – this young lady here, I mean.' He indicated my daughter, who chewed her lip and couldn't stop herself from looking pleased.

'What is he saying?' my mother demanded.

'I'll just – go away, then,' the soldier said. He seemed to be dying several thousand deaths at once.

'He'd like some tea...' my daughter told my mother. 'We'll just have a quick cup or two,' I added, and we took the tea out onto the verandah, and drank it under the eyes of God and the entire neighbourhood. The neighbourhood was annoyed. Very annoyed, and it listened closely to everything that was said. The soldier didn't seem to notice. He and my daughter were getting along famously. I didn't catch what exactly they were talking about, I just poured the tea and made sure my hand was steady. *I'm not doing anything wrong*, I told myself. *I'm not doing anything wrong.*

The scrawny soldier asked if I would tell him my name. 'No,' I said. 'You have no right to use it.' He told me his name, but I pretended he hadn't spoken. To cheer him up, my daughter told him her name, and he said: 'That's great. A really, really good name. I might use it myself one day.'

'You can't – it's a girl's name,' my daughter replied, her nostrils flared with scorn.

'Ugh,' said the soldier. 'I meant for my daughter…'

He shouldn't have spoken about his unborn daughter out there in front of everyone, with his eyes and his voice full of hope and laughter. I can guarantee that some woman in the shadows was cursing the daughter he wanted to have. Even as he spoke someone was saying, May that girl be born withered for the grief people like you have caused us.

'Ugh,' said my daughter. 'I like that sound. Ugh, ugh, ugh.'

I began to follow the conversation better. The scrawny soldier told my daughter that he understood why the boys lined the roads with anger. 'Inside my head I call them the children of Hamelin.'

'The what?' my daughter asked.

'The who?' I asked.

'I guess all I mean is that they're paying the price for something they didn't do.'

And then he told us the story of the Pied Piper of Hamelin, because we hadn't heard it before. We had nightmares that night, all three of us – my mother, my daughter and I. My mother hadn't even heard the story, so I don't know why she joined in. But somehow it was nice that she did.

★

On his second visit the scrawny soldier began to tell my daughter that there were foreign soldiers in his country, too, but that they were much more difficult to spot because they didn't wear uniforms and some of them didn't even seem foreign. They seemed like ordinary citizens, the sons and daughters of shopkeepers and dentists and restaurant owners and big businessmen. 'That's the most dangerous kind of soldier. The longer those ones live amongst us, the more they hate us, and everything we do disgusts them... these are people we go to school with, ride the subway with – we watch the same movies and play the same video games. They'll never be with us, though. We've been judged, and they'll always be against us. Always.'

He'd wasted his breath, because almost as soon as he began with all that I put my hands over my daughter's ears. She protested loudly, but I kept them there. 'What you're talking about is a different matter,' I said. 'It doesn't explain or excuse your being here. Not to this child. And don't say 'always' to her. You have to think harder or just leave it alone and say sorry.'

He didn't argue, but he didn't apologize. He felt he'd spoken the truth, so he didn't need to argue or apologize.

Later in the evening I asked my daughter if

she was still racist against soldiers and she said loftily: 'I'm afraid I don't know what you're referring to.' When she's a bit older I'm going to ask her about that little outburst, what made her come out with such words in the first place. And I'm sure she'll make up something that makes her sound cleverer and more sensitive than she really was.

★

We were expecting our scrawny soldier again the following afternoon, my daughter and I. My daughter's friends had dropped her. Even the ones she had helped find favour with the other children forgot that their new position was due to her and urged the others to leave her out of everything. The women I knew snubbed me at market, but I didn't need them. My daughter and I told each other that everyone would come round once they understood that what we were doing was innocent. In fact we were confident that we could convince our soldier of his wrongdoing and send him back to his country to begin life anew as an architect. He'd confessed a love of our minarets. He could take the image of our village home with him and make marvels of it.

　　Noura waited until our mothers, mine and hers, were busy gossiping at her house, then she came to tell me that the men were discussing how best to deal with me. I was washing clothes in the bathtub and I almost fell in.

My crime was that I had insulted Bilal with my brazen pursuit of this soldier...

'Noura! This soldier – he's just a boy! He can hardly coax his beard to grow. How could you believe –'

'I'm not saying I believe it. I'm just saying you must stop this kind of socializing. And behave impeccably from now on. I mean – angelically.'

Three months before I had come to the village, Noura told me, there had been a young widow who talked back all the time and looked haughtily at the men. A few of them got fed up, and they took her out to the desert and beat her severely. She survived, but once they'd finished with her she couldn't see out of her own eyes or talk out of her own lips. The women didn't like to mention such a matter, but Noura was mentioning it now, because she wanted me to be careful.

'I see,' I said. 'You're saying they can do this to me?'

'Don't smile; they can do it. You know they can do it! You know that with those soldiers here our men are twice as fiery. Six or seven of them will even gather to kick a stray dog for stealing food...'

'Yes, I saw that yesterday. Fiery, you call it. Did they bring this woman out of her home at night or in the morning, Noura? Did they drag her by her hair?'

Noura averted her eyes because I was asking her why she had let it happen and she didn't want to answer.

'You're not thinking clearly. Not only can they do this to you but they can take your daughter from you first, and put her somewhere she would never again see the light of day. Better that than have her grow up like her mother. Can't you see that that's how it would go? I'm telling you this as a friend, a true friend… my husband doesn't want me to talk to you anymore. He says your ideas are wicked and bizarre.'

I didn't ask Noura what her husband could possibly know about my ideas. Instead I said: 'You know me a little. Do you find my ideas wicked and bizarre?'

Noura hurried to the door. 'Yes. I do. I think your husband spoilt you. He gave you illusions… you feel too free. We are not free.'

*

I drew my nails down my palm, down then back up the other way, deep and hard. I thought about what Noura had told me. I didn't think for very long. I had no choice – I couldn't afford another visit from him. I wrote him a letter. I wonder if I'll ever get a chance to take back all that I wrote in that letter; it was hideous from beginning to end. Human beings shouldn't say such things to each other. I put the letter into an unsealed envelope and found a local boy who knew where the scrawny soldier lived. Doubtless Bilal read the letter before the soldier did, because by evening everyone but my daughter knew what I had done. My daughter waited for the soldier until it was fully dark, and I waited with her, pretending that I was still expecting our friend. There was a song she wanted to sing to him. I asked her to sing it to me instead, but she said I wouldn't appreciate it. When we went inside at last, my daughter asked me if the soldier could have gone home without telling us. He probably hated goodbyes.

'He said he would come... I hope he's alright...' my daughter fretted.

'He's gone home to build minarets.'

'With matchsticks, probably.'

And we were both very sad.

★

My daughter didn't smile for six days. On the seventh she said she couldn't go to school.

'You have to go to school,' I told her. 'How else will you get your friends back again?'

'What if I can't,' she wailed. 'What if I can't get them back again?'

'Do you really think you won't get them back again?'

'Oh, you don't even care that our friend is gone. Mothers have no feelings and are enemies of progress.'

(I really wonder who my daughter has been talking to lately. Someone with a sense of humour very like her father's...)

I tickled the sole of her foot until she shouted.

'Let this enemy of progress tell you something,' I said. 'I'm never sad when a friend goes far away, because whichever city or country that friend goes to, they turn the place friendly. They turn a suspicious-looking name on the map into a place where a welcome can be found. Maybe the friend will talk about you sometimes, to other friends that live around him, and then that's almost as good as being there yourself. You're in several places at once! In fact, my daughter, I would even go so far as to say that the further away your friends are, and the more spread out they are, the better your chances of going safely through the world...'

'Ugh,' my daughter said.

Biographical Notes

DAVID CONSTANTINE, born 1944 in Salford, Lancs, was for thirty years a university teacher of German language and literature. He has published several volumes of poetry, most recently, *Nine Fathom Deep* (2009). He is a translator of Hölderlin, Brecht, Goethe, Kleist, Michaux and Jaccottet. In 2003 his translation of Hans Magnus Enzensberger's *Lighter than Air* (Bloodaxe) won the Corneliu M Popescu Prize for European Poetry Translation. His translation of Goethe's *Faust, Part I* was published by Penguin in 2005; *Part II* in April 2009. He is also author of one novel, *Davies* (Bloodaxe) and *Fields of Fire: A Life of Sir William Hamilton* (Weidenfeld). His three short story collections are *Back at the Spike* (Ryburn), the highly acclaimed *Under the Dam* (Comma), selected by *The Guardian* and *Independent* as one of their Books of the Year, and *The Shieling* (Comma), which was shortlisted for the 2010 Frank O'Connor International Short Story Award. He lives in Oxford, where he edits *Modern Poetry in Translation* with his wife Helen.

AMINATTA FORNA is a memoirist, novelist and essayist. Her most recent published work is *The Memory of Love* (April 2010) a story about friendship, war and obsessive love. It has been selected as one of the Best Books of the Year by the *Sunday Telegraph, Financial Times* and *Times*. Her previous novel *Ancestor Stones* was a *New York Times* Editor's Choice book, selected by the Washington Post as one of the Best Novels of 2006, won the Hurston Wright Legacy Award for Debut Fiction, the Liberaturpreis in Germany and was nominated for the International Dublin IMPAC Award. *The Devil that Danced on the Water*, a memoir of her dissident father was shortlisted for the Samuel Johnson Prize 2003, serialised on BBC Radio and in *The Sunday Times* newspaper. Aminatta is a trustee of the Royal Literary Fund and sits on the advisory committee of the Caine Prize for African Writing.

SARAH HALL was born in Cumbria in 1974. She received a BA from Aberystwyth University, Wales, and a MLitt in Creative Writing from St Andrews, Scotland. She is the author of *Haweswater*, which won the 2003 Commonwealth Writers Prize for Best First Novel, a Society of Authors Betty Trask Award, and a Lakeland Book of the Year prize. In 2004, her second novel, *The Electric Michelangelo*, was short-listed for the Man Booker prize, the Commonwealth Writers Prize (Eurasia region), and the Prix Femina Etranger, and was long-listed for the Orange Prize for Fiction. Her third novel, *The Carhullan Army,* was published in 2007, and won the 2006/07 John Llewellyn Rhys Prize, the James Tiptree Jr. Award, a Lakeland Book of the Year prize, and was short-listed for the Arthur C. Clarke Award for science fiction. Her fourth novel, *How to Paint a Dead Man,* was long-listed for the 2009 Man Booker Prize.

JON MCGREGOR's first novel, *If Nobody Speaks of Remarkable Things,* was longlisted for the 2002 Man Booker Prize and went on to win the Betty Trask Prize and the Somerset Maugham Award. His second novel, *So Many Ways To Begin,* was published in 2006 and also longlisted for that year's Man Booker Prize. His third novel, *Even The Dogs,* was published by Bloomsbury in 2010. His short stories have previously appeared in *Granta, Conjunctions,* and on BBC Radio 4. He was born in Bermuda in 1976, grew up in Norfolk, and now lives in Nottingham.

HELEN OYEYEMI was born in 1984. She is the author of three novels, *The Icarus Girl, The Opposite House* and *White is For Witching,* and a short story collection, *Mr Fox,* to be published in summer 2011.